POKÉMON

BATTLE FRONTIER

GROVYLE TROUBLE

Based on the episode "Odd Pokémon Out"

ADAPTED BY TRACEY WEST

SCHOLASTIC INC.

New York   Toronto   London   Auckland   Sydney
Mexico City   New Delhi   Hong Kong   Buenos Aires

ISBN-13: 978-0-545-00562-3
ISBN-10: 0-545-00562-0

Published by Scholastic Inc.
SCHOLASTIC and associated logos are trademarks and/or registered trademarks of Scholastic Inc.

12 11 10   9 10 11 12/0

Designed by Cheung Tai
Printed in the U.S.A.

First printing, September 2007

Stampede!

Ash Ketchum looked over the ship's rails. His Pokémon, Pikachu, sat on his shoulder. Blue water sparkled below. A flock of Wingull flew in the clear sky overhead.

"Look! It's Chamomile Island!" May cried.

She sounded nervous, and Ash knew why. Ash and his friends May, Max, and Brock were exploring the Battle Frontier. May entered her Pokémon in contests whenever she could. She wanted to win a ribbon at each Contest Hall.

The next one was on Chrysanthemum Island. To get there, they'd have to board a connecting ship on Chamomile Island.

"Don't worry, May," Ash said. "We'll get there in time for the contest."

The ship docked soon after. The friends had some time before the next connecting ship came. They left the dock and gazed out onto the grassy plains of Chamomile Island.

The place was a real haven for wild Pokémon. Yellow and brown Girafarig peacefully munched on grass. Ponyta raced across the plains, their fiery manes flaming behind them.

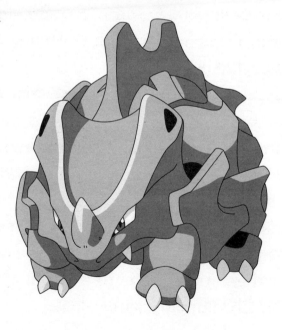

"Awesome, a herd of Rhyhorn!" Max said, pointing. Behind his glasses, his dark eyes shone with excitement.

Ash had never seen so many Rhyhorn together in one place. The tough-looking Pokémon had thick, gray skin. Each one had a sharp horn on top of its nose, and jagged ridges sticking out from its body.

"There are all kinds of Pokémon out here," Brock said, looking around.

That gave Ash an idea. "Hey, let's bring the gang out for some fun!"

"All right!" May agreed.

Ash, May, and Brock tossed out the Poké Balls they were carrying. Their Pokémon appeared in bright flashes of light.

Ash's Donphan, Corphish, Grovyle, and Swellow popped out.

Brock's Forretress, Marshtomp, and Bonsly joined them.

Then came May's Pokémon: Munchlax, Squirtle, Eevee, and Combusken.

Ash's Pikachu never traveled in a Poké Ball. The little yellow Pokémon hopped off Ash's shoulder and ran to join its friends.

With a happy cry, the Pokémon scattered across the plains.

Donphan ran up a tiny hill. The Armor Pokémon had two sharp tusks, and a thick trunk. Donphan looked tough, but had a playful personality.

Three baby Rhyhorn ran up the hill, pushing a ball made of grass. The ball rolled toward Donphan. It happily picked up the ball with its

trunk. Then it ran toward the Rhyhorn. Donphan wanted to play catch!

But the little Rhyhorn got scared. They turned and ran. Donphan didn't know they were scared, so it ran after them to play.

Then two *big* Rhyhorn charged up the hill. Their eyes glowed red with anger. They thought Donphan wanted to hurt their babies.

Surprised, Donphan skidded to a stop. The ball dropped from its trunk. Donphan spun around and ran away as fast as it could.

More Rhyhorn gave chase. Soon the ground rumbled as their heavy feet pounded the ground.

Ash felt the ground shake. He looked up and saw Donphan running toward him.

Then he saw the charging herd of Rhyhorn.

The others saw it too.

"Stampede!" they yelled.

2

Grovyle vs. Tropius

A loud car engine drowned out the sound of the stampede. Ash saw a jeep speeding toward them. The jeep cleared the top of a hill. Then it landed between Ash and the Rhyhorn herd.

Dust clouds puffed from under the jeep's tires. Nurse Joy jumped out. She faced the herd and threw a Poké Ball into the air.

"Meganium, let's go!" she yelled.

A green Pokémon burst from the ball. Big pink flower petals grew around its neck, like a collar. The Pokémon's thick body rested on four sturdy legs. It had a long neck, and two thin antennae waved on top of its forehead like thin flower stems.

"*Ganium!*" it cried.

"Meganium, use Growl now!" Nurse Joy ordered.

Meganium nodded and opened its wide mouth. An eerie sound came forth, traveling on sonic waves.

Growl hit the Rhyhorn herd. They all sank to the ground. It put them to sleep immediately.

The stampede was over.

Nurse Joy turned to Ash and his friends. "Everyone okay?"

"Thanks to you, Nurse Joy," Ash answered, smiling. Ash had traveled all over the world, and everywhere he went he saw Nurse Joy or one of her sisters. They all had pink hair and wore white uniforms. "You two were great!"

May admired Nurse Joy's Pokémon. "Wow, a Meganium," she said.

Ash flipped on his Pokédex and typed quickly.

Meganium's picture appeared on the small screen.

"Meganium, the Herb Pokémon," the Pokédex said. "Meganium's breath has the power to revive dead grass and plants. The fragrance emanating from its flower petals can soothe angry, hostile emotions."

Meganium smiled sweetly. *"Ganium!"* the Pokémon said.

Brock rushed toward Nurse Joy. He had a dreamy look in his eyes.

"Nurse Joy, you are just like Meganium," he told her. "Your ravishing beauty and gentle nature is like a refreshing breeze that blows calmly across these plains!"

Max frowned. Why did Brock have to fall in love with every female who crossed his path? He grabbed Brock by the ear.

"Too bad for you I've kept *my* anger and hostility," he said, pulling Brock away.

Nurse Joy smiled at Ash. "You've got quite a group of Pokémon there," she said. "I do hope they're feeling all right."

"Thanks!" Ash said. He scanned the Pokémon. They all looked calm after the Rhyhorn scare. "Everything looks fine to me!"

Then Ash noticed something. His Grovyle was missing!

"Hold on! Where did Grovyle go?" he asked.

Pikachu pointed to a nearby apple tree. Ash's green Grovyle stood there. Grovyle stood almost three feet tall. It had a sleek, green body with a pink underbelly. Long, green leaves grew from its wrists, the top of its head, and its tail. A brown stick dangled from its mouth. Its yellow eyes burned with determination.

A big, brown Pokémon faced Grovyle. It was more than twice the size of Grovyle, with a solid lower body and a long, thick neck. A green leaf covered the top of its head like some kind of helmet. Yellow fruit dangled from the Pokémon's

neck. Large green leaves grew out of its back. They looked like wings.

"What's going on?" Ash asked. "And who's the other guy?"

He flipped open his Pokédex.

"Tropius. The Fruit Pokémon," the Pokédex reported. "The fruit that grows around its neck is sweet and popular with children. It flies by flapping the large leaves on its body."

Ash frowned. Tropius sounded like a friendly Pokémon. But *this* Tropius was a lot bigger than Grovyle — and it looked really angry.

"*Ganium.*" Meganium sounded worried.

"Oh no!" Nurse Joy cried. "It looks like Tropius has taken over that tree as its own. So if anyone dares to come close, Tropius attacks!"

"Whoa, that's awful!" Ash wailed.

Before Ash could do anything to help Grovyle, Tropius leaped into the air. It smacked Grovyle with its wings, knocking the Grass-type Pokémon to the ground.

Grovyle jumped to its feet. But Tropius was

flapping its wings now, getting ready for a new attack.

"Grovyle, look out!" Ash warned.

Whoosh! Tropius blasted Grovyle with a powerful Gust attack. The wind sent Grovyle tumbling backward.

"Hold on, I'm coming!" Ash cried. He ran toward the tree, but the strong winds pushed him back.

Before Grovyle could recover, Tropius attacked with Razor Leaf. The sharp leaves stung Grovyle's body.

"Meganium, stop Tropius!" Nurse Joy commanded.

"Ganium!" The Pokémon nodded and then jumped into the air. It used Razor Leaf, too. The attack stunned the unexpecting Tropius.

Meganium ran up to Tropius. The big Pokémon hung its head. It looked ashamed.

"Ganium, Ganium, Ganium!" Meganium scolded.

"Wow!" Max remarked. "Meganium just stopped Tropius dead in its tracks!"

Team Rocket's Plot

3

"I've seen this before," Nurse Joy said. "For some reason, Tropius won't attack my Meganium."

Ash ran to his Pokémon. "Grovyle! Grovyle!"

The Pokémon lay in the grass, flat on its back. Its eyes were closed.

"Say something, Grovyle, please!" Ash begged.

The Pokémon's eyes fluttered. *"Gro ... vyle,"* it said weakly.

Ash's friends and Nurse Joy gathered around.

"No time to lose!" Nurse Joy said. "We've

got to get Grovyle to the Pokémon Center right away!"

Ash carried Grovyle to Nurse Joy's jeep. Everyone piled in. Then the car quickly sped away.

Tropius watched them go. It looked sad to see Meganium leave. It sighed, then began to munch apples from the tree.

Three figures watched Tropius from a nearby bush.

One was a young woman with long, magenta hair. She wore a white uniform with a red "R" on the front.

The second was a young man with bluish hair. He wore a white uniform, too.

The third was a small white Pokemon with big eyes, whiskers, and pointy brown and black ears. An oval gold jewel sat in the center of its forehead.

It was Team Rocket, of course — a trio of Pokémon thieves.

"Talk about brawn," Jessie said, admiring Tropius.

"Bravo! Tropius is feisty *and* fruit-filled," James agreed.

"Which means, it's a perfect present for the Boss!" Meowth added.

Jessie and James were shocked. "Have you flipped your script?"

"Not yet," Meowth said. "Keep what's left of your minds open and dig this!"

Meowth got a dreamy look in its eyes. It imagined Team Rocket's boss relaxing on a beach.

"Imagine the Boss lazin' around on some island under the shade of those large leaves growing out of Tropius's back," Meowth said. "And while he's being fanned by Tropius's leaves, the Boss could take a little pause for the cause by chowing down on some of Tropius's yummy fruit. And remembering who made it all possible, guess what he's gonna say?"

Meowth beamed. "He's going to say, 'Excellent! I've got to reward Meowth and his friends with a big promotion and a fat raise!'"

Jessie and James got caught up in Meowth's fantasy.

"We've been lumped up," James said.

"Now we're getting bumped up," Jessie added.

"To first class!" the two cheered together.

Jessie's eyes focused on Tropius. "Now all we have to do is log and capture."

Meowth frowned. It remembered the powerful attacks Tropius used on Grovyle. "That's easier said than done."

"Wait! Perhaps a dab of diplomacy might do the deed," James suggested.

Jessie nodded. "You're a dandy, double-talking diplomat, Meowth."

"Me? No way!" Meowth cried.

"Yes way!" James said. "Talk to Tropius. With your natural negotiating skills, it'll be eating out of your paw."

"Either that, or *eating* my paw," Meowth

mumbled. It sighed. Jessie and James wouldn't let Meowth back out now.

Seconds later, Meowth tiptoed up to Tropius. It used a megaphone so it wouldn't have to get too close.

"Uh, my name is Meowth, Team Rocket negotiator," Meowth announced. Tropius stopped munching on an apple. It looked at Meowth curiously.

"Have I got a sweet deal for you!" Meowth went on. "How'd you like anything you ever wanted? All the Pokémon food you can eat? A pillow for that big head of yours? If it exists and you want it, I can get it!"

"*Eeee?*" Tropius squeaked. It was definitely interested.

Tropius and Meowth talked for a little while. Jessie and James waited anxiously. They watched Meowth nod at Tropius.

"No problemo!" Meowth told Tropius. "I'm a can-do Pokémon and you can consider it done, dude!"

Meowth walked back to Jessie and James.

"So what does Tropius want?" James asked.

"Tropius just wants Meganium to come along, too," Meowth announced.

"What?!" Jessie and James were shocked.

"Tropius and Meganium are in love," Meowth explained.

"*Eeeee*," Tropius blushed.

"That would totally explain why Tropius stopped attacking just as soon as Meganium made the scene," Jessie realized.

"Rumor has it that Meganium have the power to heal," James said. "So if we were to gift the Boss with a package deal . . ."

"I can hear his happy squeal!" Jessie finished.

Meowth's eyes glittered at the thought of bringing *two* Pokémon to the Boss.

"Let's stop rappin' and make it real!" Meowth cried.

Grovyle in Love

Nurse Joy sped to the nearby Pokémon Center. There, Trainers could find shelter, meet other trainers, and heal their injured Pokémon.

Soon Grovyle was resting on a bed in a clean, white room. Nurse Joy, Ash, and the others surrounded the Pokémon. Meganium leaned over the bed and opened its mouth wide.

Meganium's sweet, healing breath wafted over Grovyle. The sound of soothing chimes filled the air, and a soft white light lit up the room. Grovyle immediately looked calmer and more relaxed.

"Nurse Joy, do you think Grovyle will be all right?" Ash asked, worried.

"Pikachu?" Pikachu was worried, too.

"I think so," Nurse Joy replied. "Meganium's healing powers should be strong enough to deal with Grovyle's wounds."

Grovyle opened its eyes. *"Grovyle,"* it said weakly.

Meganium smiled happily. *"Ganium!"*

Grovyle's cheeks turned red. Then something amazing happened. A flower bloomed on the end of the stick in Grovyle's mouth!

"Grovyle?" Ash asked.

"You see?" May said. "All this attention from Meganium and Grovyle's better already."

"Maybe, but it looks more like true love to me," Brock said.

Grovyle hid its face, embarrassed.

"Grovyle's going to be fine," Nurse Joy assured them. "Things will be back to normal after a bit more rest. For now, take it easy, Grovyle!"

Nurse Joy left the room, and Meganium followed her.

"Thanks, both of you!" Ash called after them.

Grovyle's face flushed as it watched Meganium walk away. Ash looked at Grovyle, concerned.

"Guys, check it out!" Ash told his friends. "Grovyle's burning up!"

"It's a fever," Brock whispered to Max and May. "A fever Grovyle got from being *love* sick!"

"Poor thing," May said. "I guess it's better than being banged up!"

"But after losing to Tropius in the first place, it didn't exactly help to build up Grovyle's confidence," Brock reminded them. "Talk about being embarrassed — no wonder Grovyle's feeling frustrated about telling Meganium its true feelings!"

May nodded. "That would explain a lot."

"After all of that, no wonder Grovyle's feeling so bad," Max added.

Ash knew how Grovyle must feel. But there wasn't much they could do for the Pokémon now. "Grovyle needs lots of sleep," Ash told his friends.

"The best thing we can do is let Grovyle rest," Brock agreed.

"Right," Ash said. "A little down time and Grovyle will be good as new!"

Ash, Brock, May, and Max left the room. Grovyle sat up in bed.

It didn't want to rest at all.

It wanted to face Tropius again!

Ash and the others walked through the halls of the Pokémon Center. Then they heard a cry.

"Meganium!" Nurse Joy shouted.

They took off running and he found Nurse Joy standing by a hole in the wall of the Pokémon Center. Something had busted right through!

"Nurse Joy, what happened?" Ash asked.

Nurse Joy looked frantic. "They stole Meganium!"

She pointed outside to where a giant metal robot towered over the Pokémon Center. It walked on two giant, metal legs and had two dangerous claws at the end of its long, metal arms. Meganium was trapped in one of the claws!

"Yeah, but who are they?" Ash wondered.

The top of the robot opened up. Jessie and James popped out.

"Prepare for trouble as we give you a peek!" Jessie said.

"And make it double, aren't I a sneak?" James asked.

Meowth popped up next. "With Meowth —"

it began, but James's Mime Jr. interrupted it. It hopped right in front of Meowth's face!

"Mime mime mime!" the cute pink Pokémon chanted.

Team Rocket continued its motto.

"Whenever there's peace in the universe . . ." Jessie began.

"Team Rocket . . ." James continued.

"Is there . . ." Meowth tried to finish, but Mime Jr. jumped in front of it again.

"Mime mime mime mime mime!" it cried happily.

"Wobbuffet!" Jessie's big, blue Pokémon chimed in.

Meowth was fuming. "Do that again and you'll be cute and *flat!*" Meowth warned Mime Jr.

Ash wasn't amused by any of these antics.

"Team Rocket!" he cried angrily, clenching his fists.

"Show's over!" Jessie said quickly. The lid to the robot closed. Then the robot stomped away across the island.

Ash broke into a run.

"Come on, hurry!" Brock yelled, running after him.

"Right!" Max and May agreed.

They chased after the robot.

They had to save Meganium!

The Rematch Begins

5

Grovyle didn't know that Meganium had been kidnapped. The Grass-type Pokémon had one thing on its mind. It wanted to beat Tropius in battle. Grovyle knew it was the only way it could face Meganium again.

Grovyle raced back to the apple tree. Tropius and Grovyle faced off once again.

"*Grovyle*," Grovyle challenged.

"*Eeeee*," Tropius replied in a low growl.

"*Grovyle*." Grovyle wanted Tropius to know it meant business.

"*Eeeee*." Tropius was ready to rumble.

Tropius made the first move. It flapped its

large wings. A powerful Gust attack swept toward Grovyle.

"Gro!" The attack sent Grovyle flying.

Tropius didn't let up. *Wham!* It pummeled Grovyle with Razor Leaf.

Grovyle shielded its face from the sharp, flying leaves. It was just like before. It didn't stand a chance against Tropius....

Then, from the corner of its eye, Grovyle saw the flower on the end of the stick. It remembered Meganium's sweet face.

That was all Grovyle needed. It jumped to its feet, and raced across the grass so quickly that Tropius didn't even see it.

Tropius stopped, confused. Where had Grovyle gone? Tropius flew through the air, looking for its opponent.

Grovyle jumped up onto a high tree branch. It watched Tropius down below.

Then, *bam!* Grovyle hit Tropius with a Bullet Seed attack. The move caught Tropius off guard. The big Pokémon stumbled.

Slash! Grovyle attacked next with Fury Cutter. Tropius fell to the ground. Then it fainted.

"Gro!" Grovyle cried triumphantly.

Then Grovyle heard a sing-song voice. "Tropius! We're home!"

Team Rocket's giant robot stomped up to the tree. The mechanical arm lowered Meganium to the ground.

"We brought Meganium, just like we promised!" Meowth called out.

"Gro?" Grovyle was confused.

So was Team Rocket.

"Hold on!" Jessie cried. "Isn't that Grovyle from the twerp's troops?"

"And why isn't Tropius jumping for joy at our return?" James wondered.

"Looks like *Tropius* got jumped instead!" Meowth remarked.

"Ganium!" A worried Meganium ran toward the tree.

Grovyle's heart began to thump. Was Meganium running toward Grovyle? It had to be true love!

Meganium ran up to Grovyle. Grovyle's cheeks burned red. It held out its arms . . .

But Meganium ran past Grovyle. It stopped next to Tropius.

"Ganium!"

"Troooo," Tropius said weakly. It couldn't lift its head.

"Ganium." A white, sparkling light shone from Meganium. The light showered Tropius.

The big Grass-and-Flying-type Pokémon felt

better. It got to its feet. Then it smiled at Meganium.

"*Troooo,*" it said, thanking Meganium.

"*Ganium!*" Meganium was very happy. The two Pokémon gently rubbed heads.

"You know, not that it matters, but don't they look kind of sweet?" Jessie said.

"Too sweet!" Meowth agreed. "Matter of fact, those two love birds go together like ketchup and fries!"

James gazed over at Grovyle. The green Pokémon hung its head sadly.

"Poor Grovyle," James remarked. "Another victim of the heart."

"Grovyle!" the poor Pokémon wailed. Grovyle fell to its knees. The flower on the end of its stick wilted and died.

Nurse Joy's jeep sped onto the scene. The jeep stopped, squealing on its brakes.

Ash jumped out of the car first. He saw his Pokémon lying on the ground.

"Oh no! Grovyle!" Ash cried.

An Amazing Evolution

6

Ash angrily glared up at Team Rocket.

"What happened?" he yelled. "What did you do to Grovyle?"

"*Pika!*" Pikachu added.

"Don't look at us!" James protested. "That's not our style."

"That was the by-product of a little bit of fisticuffs between Grovyle and Tropius," Meowth added.

Ash shook his head. "Oh man!" he exclaimed. He turned to Grovyle. "So you wanted to prove you could beat Tropius and ended up losing."

"Wake up!" Meowth cried, annoyed. "Can't

you see Grovyle beat the leaves off of Tropius, twerp?"

Ash was surprised. "Yeah? So why does Grovyle look so bummed out?"

Brock knew the answer. "It's obvious! Grovyle won the game of battle . . . but lost the game of love."

"He won *and* he lost? How do you figure that?" Ash sighed. "Brock, you've got to learn how to make up your mind."

Brock looked at Max and May and shrugged. Sometimes Ash just didn't get it.

"Courtship over," Meowth said cheerfully. He pulled a lever on the robot's control panel. "Time to haul in the happy couple!"

The two mechanical arms reached down. One metal claw grabbed Meganium. The other metal claw grabbed Tropius.

"*Ganium!*"

"*Eeeee!*"

"Quit your crying," Jessie snapped. "At least you're together!"

"Oh no!" Ash yelled.

"My Meganium!" Nurse Joy cried out.

Grovyle watched as the arm lifted Meganium into the air. The sweet Pokémon struggled to get free.

Grovyle jumped to its feet. It was angry now. It had to save Meganium.

"Grovyle!"

A bright light burst from Grovyle's body. It shimmered. Ash had to shield his eyes from the glow.

Then the light slowly faded. Now Grovyle looked completely different. It was taller, with a more muscular body. Sharp leaves grew from its arms. Its long tail was made of leaves.

"Awesome!" Ash cheered. "Grovyle's evolved into Sceptile!"

A Pokémon Without Punch

Ash checked his Pokédex to find out about his new Pokémon.

"Sceptile, the Forest Pokémon," the Pokédex said. "Its arms are equipped with razor-sharp leaves and it moves lightly through tree branches in order to attack its enemies."

"Sceptile, heads up!" Ash cried. "Go and get Tropius back!"

"*Sceeeeeept!*" Sceptile jumped high in the air, ready to attack the robot.

"We're gonna get creamed!" Meowth yelled.

Jessie and James screamed in panic.

"Seviper! Prepare for battle!" Jessie cried. She threw out a Poké Ball.

"Cacnea, you too!" James joined in. He threw a Poké Ball, too.

Meowth pulled a lever on the controls. "Time for a double dose of dynamite!"

A door on the robot's body slid open. Two Pokémon jumped up.

Seviper had a long, black body with yellow markings. Two long fangs grew from its mouth. Its tail ended in a sharp blade.

Cacnea had a round, green body. Sharp spikes stuck out of its head and its thick arms. Both Pokémon were ready to battle.

Ash made the first move.

"Now, Bullet Seed, Sceptile!" he cried.

Sceptile sprang into action. It jumped up and opened its mouth.

Nothing came out.

"Hey, no Bullet Seed!" Ash said, shocked.

"Is Sceptile sick, too?" Brock wondered.

Ash frowned. "Okay, do Leaf Blade!"

Sceptile jumped up and twirled. Sharp leaves should have flown out of its body. But nothing happened.

"*Scept?*" Sceptile was pretty confused.

Jessie, James, and Meowth burst out laughing.

"That's funny!" Meowth chortled. "I'm worried about Grovyle evolving, but all I get is a wimp!"

"Great!" Jessie said. "Time to kick Seviper up a confidence notch. Poison Tail, go!"

"*Seviper!*" The Poison-type Pokémon leapt up. *Bam!* It bashed Sceptile with its sharp tail.

"*Aaaaah!*" Sceptile moaned.

"Good show!" James cheered. "Cacnea, Needle Arm!"

Wham! Cacnea whacked Sceptile with its spiky arm. Sceptile hit the ground with a thud.

Team Rocket's Pokémon knew Sceptile couldn't fight back.

Wham!

Smack!

Bam!

They attacked Sceptile again and again.

"*Scept...*" Sceptile was too weak to move. Meowth grinned. "Now for the punch line!"

It pulled another lever on the controls. The robot's giant leg raised up. It hovered over Sceptile, ready to stomp!

8

Teamwork

"Pikachu! Aim for that machine's legs!" Ash yelled. "Thunderbolt, now!"

"Pika!" Pikachu cried. It jumped off of Ash's shoulder.

"Pikachuuuuuuuuuuuuuu!"

Pikachu's body burned with electricity. It curled its body into a tight little ball. Then . . .

Blam! A sizzling electric charge blasted the robot's legs. The metal legs began to wobble.

"We're weak in the knees!" James said.

The big robot could no longer stand. It fell backwards with a loud crash. The robot's arms swung forward. The metal claws opened up.

Meganium and Tropius jumped safely to the ground.

Nurse Joy ran up to them. "Meganium! Tropius! You're safe!" she said happily.

Team Rocket wasn't so lucky. They tumbled out of the robot's body, dirty and shaken.

"Let's get out of here before something else gets broken," Jessie moaned.

"Good thinking," Meowth agreed. He held up a small remote control device. "Of course, I just happen to be one step ahead of you!"

Meowth pressed a red button on the remote. "Goin' down!" he said.

Team Rocket's balloon floated down from the sky. The balloon had a Meowth face on it.

"Groovy, our ride's here!" James said.

Jessie, James, and Meowth jumped into the balloon basket. Seviper and Cacnea hopped in, too. Then the balloon began to fly away.

"Going up!" Team Rocket cried. "Next stop — not here!"

"Team Rocket, come back!" Ash yelled.

Sceptile stared after the balloon, helpless to stop it.

Tropius and Meganium looked at each other. They nodded.

"Eeeeeeee!" Tropius cried. It flew up into the air after the balloon.

"Ganium!" Meganium launched into Razor Leaf attack. The sharp leaves flew up toward the balloon. Then Tropius flapped its wings harder. It used Gust to send the leaves flying higher and faster.

Brock was impressed. "That Razor Leaf actually picked up power from Gust!" he remarked.

The sharp leaves sliced into the balloon. Hot air shot out. The balloon spiraled off into the distance.

"This is getting old!" Jessie complained.

"And we're not getting any younger!" James added.

"We're blasting off again!" Team Rocket shouted.

"Wobbuffet!" The blue Pokémon added.

Meganium and Tropius smiled at each other. They put their heads together and nuzzled.

"Those two were amazing together," Max said.

"What a nice couple!" May added.

Sceptile looked sadly at the two Pokémon.

It had done everything it could.

It had beaten Tropius. It had even evolved. But it couldn't save Meganium. It couldn't win Meganium's love.

Sceptile sighed.

It was no fun being the odd Pokémon out!

9

A Hundred Percent

The friends all went back to the Pokémon Center. This time, Tropius came, too. Tropius and Meganium watched the setting sun together.

"They sure look happy together," May remarked.

"Yes, and not only that, they're going to live together at the Pokémon Center," said Nurse Joy. "Isn't that nice?"

"Oh, that's so sweet," May said.

Ash was happy for Tropius and Meganium. But he couldn't stop thinking about Sceptile. After Team Rocket blasted off, he called

Sceptile back into its Poké Ball. Now he stared at the Poké Ball in his hand.

"I'm worried, Nurse Joy," he said. "Do you think Sceptile's gonna be all right?"

"Don't worry, Ash," Nurse Joy said gently. "You see, nothing's wrong with Sceptile."

Ash frowned. "If that's true, how come Sceptile couldn't do any attack moves?"

"I think it had a lot to do with a broken heart," Nurse Joy explained.

"I thought evolving fixed that," Ash said, surprised.

Nurse Joy leaned in toward the Poké Ball. "Tell me, Ash, hasn't Sceptile always been a hard worker when training with you?"

"You bet!" Ash replied. "Sceptile always gives it a hundred percent."

"Good!" Nurse Joy said. "So now you've

learned that it's not always enough to be physically strong, you know?"

Ash wasn't sure he got it.

"There are all sorts of different ways a Pokémon evolves," Nurse Joy explained. "And when you find yourself in a bind, you learn from it and grow and grow, like Sceptile's doing. And as a Trainer, you're going to grow from it, too, right?"

Ash nodded. Grovyle had learned an important lesson about itself. It needed to learn that lesson so it could evolve. Ash knew that as a Trainer, he was always learning new things about himself.

"Right!" Ash said.

"Pika!" Pikachu agreed.

"I thought so," Nurse Joy said. "And meeting good people like you is why I love my job."

Soon it was time to go. Ash, Brock, May, and Max

boarded the ship bound for Chrysanthemum Island. Nurse Joy stood on the dock with Tropius and Meganium. She waved as the ship sailed away.

"Bye Nurse Joy! Thanks a lot!" Ash called out.

"I will," Nurse Joy called back. "And May, good luck with your contest!"

"Thanks!" May answered. "I'll do my best!"

Ash looked down at his Poké Ball and smiled.

Sceptile *always* did its best for Ash. And that's really what mattered.

The ship sailed into the sunset. Ash didn't know what new adventure he would find on Chrysanthemum Island.

But whatever new challenges he faced, he knew he would do his best!